Nell of the Islands

BY MARK SCOTT

ILLUSTRATED BY RUTH BAYLEY

Acknowledgements

The Author and Illustrator appreciate the advice and assistance as our Literary Consultant, Dr Eleanor Murray Steiner whose lifetime of service and support for Highlanders and Islanders inspired this Sequel. Special thanks also to the people of Scotland's Western Isles whose daily life honours the Sea.

Nell's latest adventures could not reach her international readers and friends without the professional assistance of Andrew McKenna of Scotland's notable printers, Nevisprint of Fort William whose diligence and efficiency are self evident.

First published in Great Britain in 2005 by:
Mark Scott, Atlantic House, Island of Seil, Argyll, Scotland, PA34 4RF

Copyright © Mark Scott 2005.

Designed by Ruth J. Bayley.

Orgination, printing and binding in Scotland under the supervision of Nevisprint Ltd, Fort William, Inverness-shire, Scotland, PH33 7PH.

A catalogue record of this book is available from the British Library.

ISBN 0-9550778-0-X

Nell's Scottish Island Home...

SCOTLAND

ENGLAND

ATLANTIC HOUSE

ATLANTIC BRIDGE

AUNT KATE'S CROFT

N
W   E
S

Exploring the Islands   *and meeting Old Friends*

Dedication

*The author dedicates this Sequel to "Nell of the Seas" to his
granddaughter Ellen Sarah Steiner and also Gaia Romilly Wise,
two Children of the New Millennium, and to all New Millennium
Children, for whom both Nell books are written and
illustrated in the hope they will grow to love and honour
the Seas in the Gaelic tradition of Nach Uramach an Cuan –
How Worthy of Honour is the Sea.*

This book belongs to

Contents

Nell of the Islands

Preface

"Nell of the Islands" is the Sequel to the adventures in "Nell of the Seas" the story of Nell's journey from the stormy west coast of Scotland to sunny Australia and to her new life in a new country with new friends.

Nell's father has been a fisherman on their Scottish island home like his father and forefathers before him.

When he left Scotland to work in Australia he took Nell's mother with him. But Nell was left back on the island with her Grandfather and Grandmother until Father and Mother could find a new home for Nell and her grandparents.

When Nell and Grandma travelled by ship later to Australia, Nell found much to love in her new home and new life for the next year.

Now she starts her new adventures in "Nell of the Islands".

Bodach na Mara
The Old Man of the Seas

Chapter One

Nell's Travel Dreams

Nell awakened to the aroma of Grandma's breakfast coffee. She blinked at the dazzling Australian sunshine cascading through the open window of her waterside wooden bungalow.

Outside in the clear blue sky a snow white seagull wheeled above the seashore palm trees. The gentle waves of the incoming tide rhythmically caressed the bleached sand of the beach at the bottom of the garden. The lapping waves pulsed like the heart beat of the emerald green ocean and beat rhythmically with her own heart.

As the seagull soared away to the northern horizon, Nell closed her eyes again and dreamily remembered her beloved old island home far away on the wild, west coast of Scotland.

For the past year Nell has come to love this Australia, this new land, this new bungalow on Queensland's golden coast with all its kaleidoscopic, rainbow colours and breath catching tropical fragrances.

But all this, is no more real, no more part of Nell and no clearer for her than her fond memories of her family's old island stone house, Atlantic House that has withstood the Atlantic waves and gales sweeping across the Hebrides for over a century.

And while Grandma and Mother were busy in the kitchen, Nell recalled her old beloved Grandpa, "Skipper", alone back in Scotland, a whole world away in the cold wintry northern top of the world. Not only a whole world away from hot Australia but even in a different time zone.

For as Grandma was calling Nell to hurry for breakfast on this Friday morning, at the same time Grandpa Anderson was all alone in Scotland preparing his Thursday night supper after a hard day's fishing on the cruel waves of the icy North Sea.

Nell was startled from her recollection by her Mother knocking on the bedroom door. "Wake up Nell. You'll be late for school. Stop dawdling."

Nell wasn't dawdling because today, Friday, is one of the best days at school. Fridays are

Question Days when Teacher Mr Roberts allows any pupil to ask any question about anything.

So as she sipped her coffee, she memorised her question to Mr Roberts. He just loved teaching Geography and telling stories of his adventures in strange lands with strange sounding names on the six continents and the mysteries of the magical islands of the seven seas. He had travelled the world as a student backpacker before he became a teacher.

As Mr Roberts wiped the blackboard clean it signalled Question Time.

Nell's hand shot up – "Mr Roberts, sir, why are we here in Australia ten hours in time behind my Grandpa in Scotland?" After pausing, Nell added "When Grandma 'phones him in the morning at breakfast time, my Grandpa is having his supper at night in the dark. How is that?"

A mischievous boy at the back of the class, Peter, called Pixie Peter, because he had pointed ears, laughed "Maybe your Grandpa can't tell the time" and the classmates giggled.

Nell blushed with embarrassment and glowered at Pixie Peter. Mr Roberts rebuked him saying "Peter, you don't know a good question when you hear one."

And when the class stopped laughing at Peter, the teacher congratulated Nell on the best question of the month and he presented her with the Best Question Prize of a World Atlas.

He said he would give a lesson one day about the world's different Time Zones in the northern and southern hemispheres of the globe "up there" in Europe and "down under" in Australia.

After school Nell hurried home and excitedly told Mother and Grandma about her prize. They were all so happy until Father arrived home early. He is looking very serious and miserable, Nell thought as he looked anxiously at each one of the family. Her strong upright father now looked downcast, faltering and hesitant. Grandma asked him why he was upset.

He explained he had lost his job – the company will be closing down and there would be no more work for him. He didn't know if he would be able to find another job.

Mother was clearly upset as she wiped away her tears. "Oh Jack, what are we to do?" Father put his hand on her shoulder reassuringly and said "We must go home, back to Scotland. Back to my old job helping Grandfather with the fishing." And he explained that his company would pay for them all to return on a passenger ship from Australia to Britain.

Grandma stopped stirring her tea, stood up and briskly announced "Never mind. Never mind." She repeated: "If that's what we've got to do, we shall do it. Cheer up. We're homeward bound to Bonnie Scotland."

With that she marched to the kitchen to make another pot of tea.

But Nell did not cheer up – she felt trembly and confused. She wasn't sure if she was sad for poor Father and sad to be leaving her new home or happy to be going back to her old home and her old friends and Grandpa. She wasn't sure of anything now. It was as if she had lost an Australian dollar and found a Scottish pound.

She would miss Australia's bright sunshine, the warm blue seas, golden beaches, the bright tropical flowers and the strange bird songs and unusual animals, the kangaroos and koala bears. She would miss fresh fruit, picking of peaches, grapes and nuts with her new friends and fishing and snorkelling on the Great Barrier Reef with her special friend Fergus and his grandfather Mr MacSporran, Granfer Mac.

All these joys and delights would be forsaken – abandoned.

But she would not miss Australia's terrible storms that had killed Fergus' parents or the blistering sunburn and the bush fires. She didn't like the snakes, poisonous jelly fish, crocodiles and all the flies that sometimes gave her nightmares unlike her lovely dreams of her island back home.

She frowned at leaving Australia but smiled at the prospect of returning to Atlantic House. Back home to the Island of Birches, to Ellenabeich, and back to her old school friends and the snow capped mountains, purple heather clad glens and the soft west coast rain. It made her feel homesick as well as sad.

Grandma was too proud to ever admit she was homesick for Atlantic House and Grandpa – instead, she hid her feelings by bustling about the house and being cheerful and saying "Never mind. Never mind."

In the past year Nell had missed old Grandpa with his white beard, his sea-captain's cap, his threadbare jersey and his salty sea boots – even the blue tobacco smoke of his smelly pipe.

When the family left to go to Australia, Grandpa stayed behind to look after their old island home and to work as the Ferryman until he would retire and he too could go to Australia. He also wanted to live and die like his forefathers on the island where everyone called him

"Skipper." He would say "While I'm above the waves I am master of my fate, the Captain of my soul – after that I want to be buried at sea because I'm a seaman."

When Father went to work in Australia, Skipper said he would wait at home, saying he knew to be sure they would return one day. And he was right – How did he know she would return? Did he have the famous Highland Second Sight of prophesy?

Nell remembered Skipper sitting by the fireplace where he could cast logs on the blazing hearth or stroke his straggly beard and tell tales of the sea and olden times, before the cottages and crofts had electric lights and spin driers to dry the rain sodden clothes. Grandma didn't let him come into the house wearing his soggy sea boots and wet oilskins or smoke his smelly pipe in the house.

Nell was eager to see Skipper again and hear his soft, deep voice reciting Scottish mysteries and Gaelic legends. Her favourite tales by Grandpa were of the "Old Man of the Seas", the Scottish legends of the "Bodach Na Mara", "the Spirit of the Oceans" as the fisher folk on the grey rocky Western Islands called him.

The Bodach taught the Islanders who had ears to hear and minds to learn of the ancient Gaelic folklore "Nach uramach an Cuan" or in English "How worthy of honour is the Sea".

The Bodach explained to the islanders how to trust in themselves – how to trust their hopes if their hopes are ever to come true. And Grandpa always said while everyone is free to dream, our dreams are not free, because we must help our dreams to come true.

Grandpa told Nell that he had learned from the Old Man of the Seas during his long life that everything happens for a reason and in time we can come to understand that reason even if that reason takes a long time.

After the shock of Father's bad news about losing his job with all the disappointment and disturbance of the day, Nell lay in bed drowsily gazing at the Southern Cross of the Australian night sky.

As she closed her eyes and sighed gently, Nell felt in her heart and also knew in her head that she could trust her hopes and ambitions. She would not let her dream become a nightmare. After all she is an Islander, like Grandpa and the family and Islanders are independent and trusty.

So she slowly, sleepily slid into slumberland across the seas to the Western Isles and her dreams as "Nell of the Islands."

Farewell Party

Next morning Nell was awakened early by Grandma, Father and Mother Anderson over breakfast discussing their plan to move from Queensland 14,000 miles across the world's oceans and the great continents back to Scotland.

Father's employers, the Fisheries Department who no longer had any work for him, arranged and paid for the family's return voyage to Britain by ship from Australia's great port of Sydney.

Grandma and Mother were organising the packing of their belongings while Father went to tell the Schoolmaster and Postmistress of their leaving.

Nell's duty was to inform all their Australian friends of the departure. First was the Andersons' old Scottish friend Mr Angus MacSporran, "Granfer Mac" and his grandson Fergus who lived in their ramshackle wooden fisherman's hut along the seashore.

Then to the Church to the Minister, the Reverend Black, next to the library and then to Nell's special friends the Aboriginal cousins Billy Boy and Sally Wren whose native ancestors were Australia's first people. Next on to school friends Dolly Cook and Fearless Freddie.

Mr Mac and Fergus were very upset at Nell's news. So upset that both MacSporrans hurried along the shoreline to the Andersons' bungalow.

Over Grandma's afternoon tea and scones, Granfer Mac admitted to Grandma and Father that he was getting older and also because Fergus wanted to see Scotland Mr Mac had been thinking for a long time about returning to his "ane hame" in Scotland so Fergus could go to a Scottish school like his MacSporran ancestors before him. Granfer Mac also wanted to meet his Scottish cousin Kate again. This pleased Grandma because she knew the two cousins had not seen each other for years.

After long talks over the following days with the Andersons, Mr Mac decided to sell his wooden shack and furniture as well as his fishing boat for the money to pay for the voyage back to Scotland with the Andersons.

'Haste ye back'

Happy to meet, Sorry to part
Happy to meet again

13

Meantime Nell and Fergus discussed their own plans for Scotland. They would visit old castles, go to Highland Games and Clan Gatherings in the glens with kilted Highlanders playing bagpipes – especially of the Anderson and MacSporran Clans. Fergus and Granfer would stay with Granfer's cousin Miss Katherine MacSporran, "Kate" at her island home, the Croft. Nell explained Kate is an artist and is Grandma's friend.

They would sail in Grandpa's boat over the sea to Skye and sing the Skye Boat Song "Speed Bonnie Boat like a bird on the wing" which Nell taught Fergus who quickly learned it.

Nell told him about Shetland ponies, the long horned shaggy Highland cattle, the eagles hovering over the mountain peaks of Ben Nevis and Ben More and deer stags.

Fergus was impatient to know about snow. He had never seen snow and urged Nell to explain why it was different from rain, how to make snowballs and snowmen as well as how to ski on the slippery white stuff.

She also told him about her white pet rabbit "Snowy". Fergus thought that she was daft because no one kept pet rabbits in Australia where they are so common they are a nuisance – just like all the flies in Australia.

They both agreed that life would be very different in Scotland with the cold winters, rainy days and Scotch mist and breakfast porridge, scones and marmalade, hot meat pies and Scotch broth with homemade bread.

"But honestly, Fergus" Nell told him "You'll be alright on our west coast – Really you will."

Fergus nodded thoughtfully – "I believe you Nell. I want to see Granfer's birthplace. And I want to go to school to be as clever as you Nell." This surprised her. They were friends because they respected each other as well as liking one another. "You know Fergus" she said "You are clever in your own way. We just know different things. And I want to be as clever as you. So we'll help each other with our homework."

They both laughed together and ran back to help Granfer Mac with his packing.

On the way, Nell suddenly stopped walking. She told Fergus they must write to their Swiss friend Jan and tell him they were leaving Australia to move to Scotland. Fergus agreed. He liked Jan whom he had met in Australia and enjoyed the adventures with Nell and Jan as "The Crew of Three".

The Andersons and MacSporrans assisted each other and everything went well for their departure – even the Farewell Bar-B-Q organised by all their friends of the past year.

Lots of people came to say their Goodbye's and Bon Voyage as well as to hear Father Jack blow his bagpipes while Granfer Mac played the fiddle and Grandma and Mother sang Scottish folksongs.

As the party was ending Grandma announced it would not be a proper Scottish party – or a "Ceilidh" as Scots call it, if the company did not say together the traditional Scottish Farewell:- "Happy to meet, Sorry to Part, Happy to meet again".

Then Mr Mac and Father played the music of Auld Lang Syne and Grandma and Mother sang the words "Should auld acquaintance be forgot and never brought to mind? Should auld acquaintance be forgot, for auld lang syne".

Mr Mac told his Australian neighbours he wanted to leave them with a Celtic blessing:- "May the road rise up to meet you. May the wind be always at your back. May the sun shine warm upon your face. May the rain fall soft upon your field. And until we meet again, May God hold you in the Palm of His Hand".

Everyone cheered and shouted their best wishes for "Godspeed for a Safe journey" and added the Scots farewell "Haste ye back".

As Nell and Fergus walked home Fergus told Nell that they must also write to Jan about the party, their Farewell Bar-B-Q.

May the road rise up to meet you.
may the wind be always at your back.
may the sun shine warm upon your face.
may the rain fall soft upon your field.
and until we meet again ~
may God hold you in the Palm of his hand.

Chapter Three

Homeward Bound-Speed Bonnie Boat

Grandma and Mother organised the removal packing in the neat and tidy way that women do. Father wrote the luggage labels while Mr Mac and Fergus carried the cases and Nell made pots of tea.

Everything went well for the Andersons and the MacSporrans, whom Grandma decided to call "The Islanders". When they arrived at the Airport to fly to the great Port of Sydney to join their ship, Mr Mac seemed quiet and unhappy. "He's sulking. Just because he can't smoke his smelly pipe in the airplane." Grandma snapped. For once Mr Mac did not answer back but just remained silent even when Fergus whispered "What's the matter, Granfer?"

Mother May, who had been a nurse, was very fond of Granfer Mac. Only she, like Fergus, called him "Granfer" because he reminded Mother of her own Grandfather who died long ago. Mother sat close beside the old man and talked quietly to him. He whispered to her "You know May, I've never been up in a 'plane. I don't like heights. I'm scared to be high in the sky." Mother patted his hand relaxing him in the 'plane seat. Sitting close to him, Mother squeezed Granfer's arm and asked him to close his eyes and relax. Then she asked Granfer to remember the happiest day when he was a young laddie in Scotland long ago and to imagine a future happy day with Fergus back on the island. Mother kept reassuring him in her soft, soothing Highland voice as the engines roared and the 'plane rose like a silver eagle up to the skies.

Mr Mac closed his eyes tighter and gripped Mother May's arm. "It's alright Granfer" she encouraged him. "You can open your eyes now. We're on our way home to Bonnie Scotland."

Mr Mac slowly lifted one eyelid and saw all "The Islanders" were relaxed and smiling.

The Air Hostess patted Granfer's shoulder saying "It's very nice having you with us, Mr MacSporran."

And Grandma leaned across to him and said "Never mind, Angus, it's nice up here."

Mr Mac nodded as he remembered that Grandma had once told him that she didn't like flying because she didn't like heights as she didn't have wings! But she also told him she had flown in a 'plane after she arrived in Australia and it was thrilling.

Grandma looked happy and she told Granfer Mac "Look out the window now, Angus. It's lovely."

Mr Mac leaned forward very slowly and gingerly peeked out of the porthole. Then he leaned closer and even closer and rubbed the glass with his hand. He looked quite excited as he stared out at the blue sky and fluffy white clouds around him and the Blue Mountains below him.

The old man gasped in amazement. "I'm in heaven" he exclaimed "I've died and I'm up in heaven." He pulled his ear and said to Mother "Thank you May my dear, I'm alright now. This is grand." Grandma, Nell and Mother all smiled kindly at Mr Mac. Fergus was proud of his brave Granfer who had the courage to face his fear of flying and had conquered his fear. Grandma always liked the last word and said "I told you Angus – flying is fun."

After their 'plane flew over the Blue Mountains and landed at Sydney Airport, "The Islanders" spent the day exploring the exciting city. Father Jack said "To think it was a convict settlement after Captain Cook landed at Sydney's Botany Bay."

"The Islanders" each wanted to explore the City's Opera House, the great Harbour Bridge and sample meals in the city's different restaurants of the 200 different nationalities in the international city.

But Grandma Anderson had planned a real surprise. After buying a bunch of flowers from a street vendor, she bundled "The Islanders" into a big Taxi. She explained that she was taking them on a special visit, a pilgrimage to honour Nell's famous Scots ancestor, Sir Francis Anderson. He was Nell's great, great, great Uncle who was born in Glasgow, Scotland in the 19th Century, graduated Master of Arts from Glasgow University in 1883 and in 1888 emigrated to Australia as a lecturer in Philosophy and became Vice Chancellor of Sydney University.

When they arrived at Sydney's world-famous University, Grandma marched them all to a quadrangle. There was the Sir Francis Anderson Memorial Fountain cascading cool sparkling water in the hot afternoon sun. Grandma placed the flower bouquet at the fountain with its stone inscription which said "Sir Francis Anderson, Professor of Logic and Mental Philosophy 1890-1921."

Then the Anderson family held hands, Grandma, Jack, May and Nell Anderson while Grandma said a quiet tribute to their ancestor, the young Scottish student who became an Australian and a World famous Peace Maker for the League of Nations. Mr Mac photographed the Andersons gathered at the Anderson Fountain and Fergus picked out a pebble from the waterfall as a souvenir to take back to Scotland.

Then "The Islanders" all tumbled back into the Taxi and raced to the harbour to catch their ship, past places with Scottish names like McQuarrie St., Argyll Place, MacDonald and Campbells' Cove and the 2000 Olympic Stadium.

Even before they reached the dockside, they could see the huge Cruise Ship with its massive funnel, towering over the harbour. It was even larger than the liner on which Nell and Grandma had sailed from Britain to Australia a year ago.

Fergus and Mr Mac were astonished at the size of the great white floating city. "You never told me it would be so big" Fergus said to Nell. And Mr Mac joined in saying "Jeannie Anderson, it's like a grand hotel floating in the sea."

Grandma chuckled "Aye it is, Angus MacSporran. And when you are aboard you'll think you are in heaven again." Mr Mac believed her until he saw the "No Smoking" signs and he put his pipe away again in his pocket.

The ship's steward quickly ushered them and their luggage to their cabins, Father and Mother to theirs, Nell and Grandma in another and Fergus and Granfer opposite across the corridor. All the cabins were like luxury hotel rooms with a television, telephone, fridges and everything to make them comfortable.

Then "The Islanders" joined the rest of the 2000 passengers on the top deck to watch the great ship slip her moorings and gently part from the dockside as if the Liner was kissing farewell to Australia to the mournful moan of the ship's siren.

As the Liner floated away from the harbour to the ocean, everyone waved and cheered her "Farewell, Godspeed" on her world voyage home.

Grandma touched Mr Mac's arm and began softly singing the old Scottish folk song – "Speed bonnie boat, like a bird on the wing, over the sea to Skye".

Nell and Fergus thought they saw tears in their Grandparents' eyes. Fergus put his arm on Nell's shoulder and whispered to her: "We shall

SIR FRANCIS ANDERSON

PROFESSOR OF LOGIC
& ORIENTAL PHILOSOPHY
1890-1921

Photograph for Grandpa

come back one day, won't we Nell?" She nodded "Yes, Fergus. We'll come back one day."

Mr Mac was waving his farewell to his adopted Australia. He explained a man can have two countries, he can love two lands – first his birth land of his forefathers and second his adopted homeland of his new home and new family. Fergus nodded in agreement. Like Granfer he belonged to both lands, Australia, his birthland and Scotland his ancestral homeland.

The ship surged on seawards like a high walled stately Castle of the Ocean on her long voyage over the world's stormy seas. She would steam across the Equator and the latitudes and longitudes, those invisible lines that criss cross the globe. Like signposts they help the ships' navigators to chart their voyages over the unmarked seas to the other side of the world. She would sail to the hot and cold continents, to the exciting exotic islands in the warm Pacific and the blue Caribbean oceans and then into the cold cruel Atlantic ocean beating wild winds and fierce waves to reach "The Islanders'" home, the British Isles.

They were leaving the world's greatest island, the continent of Australia which is surrounded by different seas and which was discovered by seafarers and explorers from Britain.

New Zealand and a Strange Birthday

Three days after leaving Australia the Liner dropped anchor in a country made up of two separate North and South islands of New Zealand in the South Pacific Ocean.

New Zealand, the home of the curious kiwi birds with no wings, of sweet kiwi fruits, the homeland of the fierce looking but friendly Maori peoples, the islands of scenic mountains, volcanoes, glens, lakes and rolling countryside with flocks of New Zealand lamb and herds of dairy cattle for making New Zealand butter.

Nell felt at home because New Zealand reminded her of Scotland with Scottish place names like MacDougal, Murray and MacDonald. Their forebears had left the Scottish Highlands and Islands long ago and cleared the bushland, while fishermen harvested shoals of fish and the beautiful and rare paua shells for exotic jewellery.

But the highlight of their New Zealand visit was an invitation to a real Maori native village at Rotorua in a valley of hot water springs. It was a place of surprises – where the earth rumbles and growls while it throws up pools of plopping mud and sparkling geysers of hot water and puffing steam from the volcanoes deep below the earth.

At the village a proud Maori guide welcomed "The Islanders" in true Maori tradition. Then he embraced Grandma and rubbed noses with her. Grandma blushed and said "Oh dear, dearie me. What would my friend Kate and the neighbours say?" Everybody laughed. They had never before seen Grandma so shy and lost for words.

The Guide then rubbed noses with all the other visitors and invited them all to a Maori feast, and a Maori concert and tribal display.

The feast was delicious but the Tribal Display was scary. The fierce warriors shook their spears and stamped their feet for their thundering Hakka war dance. Worse still, they all stuck out their tongues while they shook their spears and roared. Grandma, Mother May and Nell tried to hide behind Mr Mac, Father Jack and Fergus.

But the huge tattooed Warrior called the "Maori Mountain Man" spotted Grandma and before she could run away the fierce Warrior lifted her up and after rubbing her nose put out his tongue but then smiled and wished her "Kia Ora" – "Long Life." Next he presented her with a precious paua brooch. Poor Grandma didn't know whether to faint with embarrassment or clap her hands and jump for joy, so she politely shook hands with the Gentle Giant and wished him the gaelic "Slainte mhath" or "Good Health".

To recover from her fright with the frightful "Maori Mountain Man", a lovely, kind Maori lady invited Grandma to Afternoon Tea. Mother May and Nell went to the village to watch the Maori craftsmen creating the rare and special Maori paua jewellery while Mr Mac, Father and Fergus watched the tribal craftsmen carving intricate wooden objects of beauty from logs.

The Tour Guide shepherded them on to the Tour Coach to return to Auckland to rejoin the ship.

After everyone was aboard, the Liner steamed at full speed ahead during the night towards the Equator, to the warm South Pacific, to the South Sea Polynesian islands and the tropical island of Tahiti.

The Scottish Islanders were all tired after their long day with the friendly Maoris, so Grandma ordered everybody early to bed – especially as the next day, the 5th March was the 12th birthday of Fergus.

During the night, while all the passengers were asleep in their snug cabins, the Captain and his navigator were wide awake on the ship's bridge. On the night watch, they steered the great Liner through the darkness across the Pacific Ocean.

As dawn broke, the ship crossed longitude 172°30′W.

After breakfast, Fergus excitedly opened his birthday cards and presents, a watch from Granfer, a World Atlas Globe from Grandma, a telescope from Father Jack and Nell's pocket compass. Mother May presented him with a Big Book on "The Weather". Mother and Fergus liked chatting together about the weather. Mother knew he was interested in Meteorology and weather forecasting because his own mother and father had died in a terrible storm in Australia. Mother May had wanted to be a Meteorologist instead of a nurse but then she was unable to go to University, so now she liked learning about weather with Fergus.

At his Birthday Party in the ship's dining room, the patisserie Chef produced a real surprise for Fergus! A blue and white iced Birthday Cake with 12 candles and "Happy Birthday" written in blue icing sugar with a Scottish Saltire flag.

But the biggest birthday surprise of all and the most amazing present anyone could receive came from the Captain the next day, March 6th.

Over the ship's loudspeaker system, the Captain announced "Attention please. This is the Captain. We have sailed across the International Date Line and have crossed longitude 172 degrees West. We now have to retard, to put back the ship's clocks by 24 hours and this takes us onto Greenwich Meantime minus eleven hours.

This means that while yesterday was the first Wednesday 5th March, today is now the second Wednesday 5th March. So believe it or not, we have two days with the same date in the same week of the same year." The passengers looked puzzled and shook their heads in disbelief.

Grandma whispered to Mother May "I hope we don't have to pay two days' fare for one day." Mother muttered "Don't be silly."

Then the Captain announced in his serious Captain's voice "This also means that Master Fergus MacSporran who had his 12th birthday yesterday can now have another birthday today as well. Congratulations Fergus. Happy Birthday again to you."

Everyone clapped and cheered – except Fergus who just looked embarrassed and puzzled. "Does this mean I am one or two years older?" he asked. Father Jack, who understood navigation replied "No, no. Although you have had two birthdays you are only one year older." And Nell added "So you won't get two lots of birthday presents either."

Nell wished she had heard her teacher's talk to explain the world's Time Zones before she had to leave school. She asked Father to explain and he told them that, because the Earth turns round, the Sun rises in eastern countries before it rises in countries further to the west.

The new day begins first at the International Date Line, an imaginary line which goes through the Pacific Ocean from north to south (at longitude 180 degrees). Going round the Earth from east to west, the new day begins 6 hours later in parts of India, 12 hours later in Britain, 18 hours later in parts of America and 24 hours later just before arriving back at the Date Line.

When a ship sails eastwards across the Date Line, which is what happens when you are sailing from Australia to South America, its clocks go back by 24 hours and you get to have the same day twice.

Granfer Mac who listened intently smiled approvingly and said "so when a child in the east, like China, greets the rising sun, at the same time a child in the west, like America, is saying "Goodnight".

At the end of the day when Fergus went to bed he said "You know Granfer, it's the funniest birthday I've ever had. Two birthdays in two days. But I don't feel two years older."

After falling asleep Fergus dreamed of the next island on the voyage and his next birthday in Scotland.

CHAPTER FIVE

Lost on an Exotic Island - Tahiti

When Fergus awakened in his cabin he peered out of the porthole to see the Liner steaming full speed ahead in the Pacific Ocean. Ahead were the islands of French Polynesia and Tahiti. Fergus remembered his school history of how Captain Bligh sailed "The Bounty" to Tahiti 200 years ago to collect breadfruit for the West Indies. Then the crew of "The Bounty" mutinied and set Captain Bligh adrift in a small boat in the vast ocean.

Fergus hurried to the top deck where Nell and the other passengers were marvelling at the green forested island in the turquoise sea.

At the dockside of the port of Papeete everyone excitedly disembarked to explore the famous island.

The adults toured the tropical gardens with flowers of flaming colours and the Museum of Paintings of Paul Gauguin the French Artist who went to live on Tahiti and painted the natives of the island in vivid colours. Mother May stood staring at the paintings practising her French saying "C'est magnifique". Fergus got bored and he and Nell went to the jungle to see the giant bamboo trees which grow 20 inches each day and grew in front of their eyes.

Father escorted them all to an al fresco buffet lunch at a seashore palm hut restaurant. Everyone helped themselves to a sumptuous banquet of honey baked chicken, albacore fish, breadfruit and exotic vegetables before desserts of fresh mangoes, guavas and other nuts and fruits and glasses of coconut milk and fruit juices. As they feasted they threw titbits to the turquoise and black fish swimming in the emerald waters at their feet.

After lunch, Grandma and the adults went bargain hunting to the pavement stalls of the open market to buy Tahitian black pearls, wood carvings and tropical flower perfumes.

Nell and Fergus slipped away to explore Papeete's busy waterfront harbour to meet the local fishermen and traders. They soon forgot time and place. And quickly became lost. Lost among crowds of barefoot children and beggars in the bustling back streets. After hurrying and scurrying among the throng in the busy, smelly alleys they at last found their way back to the market place to rejoin Grandma and the family.

But the adults were not there! They were gone! But where? Nell was worried. It was late in the afternoon and the stall holders and fishermen were leaving town to go home to their shanty huts.

Fergus remembered their ship was due to depart with the tide before sunset and sail away across the sea.

"We must catch the ship before she sails or we will be trapped here with no money, no family, no friends and no help" said Nell. Fergus looked worried too. "It won't be so bad if Granfer and Grandma are stranded here as well because they will know what to do. But where are they?" Nell shook her head muttering "Maybe they've gone back to the ship or maybe they're lost looking for us."

Fergus wasn't listening but was looking about at the beggars and old sailors standing around the dirty old harbour pub. He remembered Robert Louis Stevenson's book "Kidnapped" and was looking even more worried. "Do you think we could be kidnapped here and held for ransom in the jungle?" he said. Nell scowled "Don't be silly Fergus. Who would want to kidnap us?" Fergus still looked worried. "But what if Granfer and your Father can't pay the ransom and free us from the jungle den?"

Nell was exasperated. "Stop it, Fergus – just

'cos you are scared, don't try to scare me." Fergus retorted "I'm not scared. I'm just worried. I don't want to miss the boat and be kidnapped. What if your folk can't find the ransom money and what if…" He suddenly stopped talking when he saw Nell looking startled, frightened at something

behind him. Fergus whirled around and he too was frightened.

A gang of local youths blocked their way. They were smoking cigarettes and twirling clapper sticks.

"What do you want?" shouted Nell "We haven't got any money."

The big Gang Leader showed his broken front tooth and puffed his cigarette. "Don't be scared Missy" he grinned, "We'll help you." Fergus interrupted him. "No, just go away." Nell added "We just want to get back to our ship."

The Gang Leader showed his broken tooth again when he said to his pals. "Do you hear that guys? They're lost." The Gang all laughed until their leader stopped them and said to Nell "Don't be scared Missy. We'll take you back to the ship. Follow us." And he turned and walked away from the jungle towards the harbour. So Nell and Fergus followed the boys through the dirty back street when Nell suddenly spotted the great ship's towering smoke funnel high above the harbour buildings. "That's our ship" shouted Nell. The Gang started running towards the Liner with Nell and Fergus breathlessly following them to where the ship's crew were waiting for the passenger stragglers.

Fergus thanked the Gang Leader who just laughed and said "Don't get lost again" and he and his pals ran away back to the town.

The Ship's Officer hustled Nell and Fergus aboard and told them "You're lucky we didn't leave you behind. We're weighing anchor now."

The ship's siren then hooted a farewell to Tahiti and steamed seaward.

"I hope Granfer and the family got back as well" said Fergus. They did. And there were Grandma, Granfer, Mother and Father standing at the ship's rail half frowning disapproval and half smiling with relief. Grandma wagged her finger at them and said "Thank Goodness you're back safely. We thought you had returned to the ship before us. Don't get lost again." And Granfer tweaked Fergus' ear and said "No supper for you tonight laddie."

Now that "The Islanders" were all reunited, they stood on the top deck to watch the glorious pink and orange coloured sunset with the quarter moon over the island peaks as the Liner steamed to the next island of Bora Bora.

It was all so heavenly that Granfer mellowed and let Fergus have supper after all, while he and Nell were scolded by the adults for their misadventures on Tahiti, the island of adventures.

CHAPTER SIX

Rescued from Sharks - Bora Bora

As the ship surged across the South Seas, Nell and Fergus studied the World Atlas to follow the Captain's course to the Leeward Islands and Bora Bora. The island, this Pearl of the South Seas, is so small that it was hard to find on Fergus' world globe.

But as they approached they saw the island's high mountain peak with its mantle of tropical forests crowned with white clouds, more like a green jewel than a pearl in the warm azure sea under a blue sky. The white soft beaches were like talcum powder. And it was so hot that some golden skinned Bora islanders sat beneath the shady palm trees among brilliant tropical flowers. Others stood under their large straw hats in the warm sea catching parrot or butterfly fish or snorkelling for shellfish.

Grandma soon lounged under a cool palm tree sipping coconut milk and watching Granfer talking to a fisherman casting a fine net to catch small fish as bait for the local fishermen's big fish. Mother watched the island housewives cooking their national dish of fafa chicken cooked with spinach and coconut milk with banana and pumpkin dessert. Father went snorkelling to see the giant stingrays and turtles.

While the adults were amusing themselves in their own way, Fergus and Nell swam in the shallow coral waters until they found an old palm log which they sat on and paddled with their hands about the coral islet like a canoe. They were so excited watching the colourful coral fish they did not notice the tide was receding from the island.

Suddenly Nell yelled "Fergus – A shark! There's a shark, a shark – Look – a shark!" as a long black tipped shark zoomed straight towards them. Fergus instantly reacted and frantically splashed the water with his arms and legs to frighten the sinister monster. Nell shrieked "Go away, leave us alone. Go away." But the fearless shark came closer and closer to the log and silently circled around them.

Grandma heard the shouts and hurried down to the beach while Granfer and the fishermen all jumped in a boat to rescue the children. Father stopped snorkelling and swam hastily towards the log. Grandma shouted "Hurry, hurry, the shark will eat them" and she tried to throw pebbles at the circling shark. But the log continued drifting out with the ebb tide further from the shore.

"Lie down on the log Nell" Fergus said "the shark won't see us if we lie down."

But there wasn't enough space on the log so Fergus kept splashing the water to stop the shark coming closer.

Granfer and the fishermen were rowing the boat as fast as they could while Father bravely swam closer to the rescue and Grandma continued shouting "Hurry, hurry."

But as the five feet long black shark circled nearer around the drifting log, Nell watched in horror as two more sinister sharks swam closer. "Keep splashing. Splash harder" yelled Nell at Fergus who was becoming exhausted by his arm waving to drive away the fearful beasts while Nell paddled with her hands against the tide.

As Granfer and the fisherboat came closer, the fishermen shouted and beat the water with their oars as they came alongside the log. Nell and Fergus scrambled into the boat and the safety of Granfer's arms. Although the sun was blazing hot, Nell and Fergus were shivering with fright.

Still the three sharks prowled around as the fishermen rowed back to the beach where Grandma welcomed their safe return and Mother came running along the beach.

One of the Bora fishermen comforted the ladies, telling them that black tipped sharks are harmless. "They look fierce but they don't eat people. They come to the lagoon for food. Don't worry. Enjoy your holiday."

The family and their Bora friends all sat down on the beach and watched the three sharks swim around the log which was being swept out to the ocean depths.

That night in the comfort of her cosy cabin Nell dreamed of sharks while Fergus stared out of his porthole scanning for sea monsters as the Liner sailed on.

"Did I do the right thing Granfer?" he asked. Granfer patted the lad's shoulder. "Never go on a log or an inflatable without paddles. But Fergus you faced your fear and kept the sharks away. Lots of things are stronger than fear, like the courage to face the fear and laughing at the fear."

Granfer smiled and added "Next stop is Hawaii. Let's hope you don't get into trouble there." Fergus nodded – hopefully.

Nell and Fergus Rescue a Lady - Hawaii

In Hawaii, Nell told Fergus "I don't see how we can get into trouble here – it's so peaceful and lovely." Fergus pointed to a Hawaiian Welcome sign reading "The two days of the week that do not matter are yesterday and tomorrow. The only day that matters is today".

Nell smiled and pointed to another Welcome sign saying "Take time to smell the flowers" and another "Live to be happy – Enjoy life".

Then a beautiful Hawaiian lady in a grass skirt and flowers in her black hair welcomed them with an "Aloha" – Greeting and placed a Leis garland of flowers around the children's necks saying "Live Life".

They didn't see any sharks off the beaches but they did see whales in the bay. They also met lots of Hawaiian folk who all call each other "cousin" even if they are not related.

Grandma and Mother walked around a pineapple plantation and admired the roadside flowers of blue jacaranda, red tiger-claw trees, frangipani and giant agapanthus and flowers many times larger than the same plants in Scotland. A fruit seller explained that Hawaii has only two seasons, dry and wet and no winter or summer – it's like summer all year.

Granfer and Father took Nell and Fergus on a bus tour of the island. The driver named Jerry called each passenger "Cousin". The coach stopped at village stalls for the "cousins" to buy fresh pineapple slices, macadamia nuts and packets of coffee beans and herbs for Grandma and Mother. They also sampled delicious rich coconut pudding and fresh fruit salads.

The sunshine was so hot that Jerry drove the bus up the twisting rocky road to Mount Haleakala volcano, the highest point of Hawaii, which was so high Nell shivered in the cold mountain air. Fergus said volcanoes were underground fires that exploded red hot molten lava. Although Jerry explained the volcano had not exploded for two hundred years, the passenger "cousins" stayed in the warm bus – just in case there was another eruption! And they

were all glad when Jerry drove down to the tropical rain forest valleys.

Down in the green moss and fern covered valley the "cousins" went walkabout through the National Park. "We mustn't get lost again so we will stay near the bus" said Fergus.

When the bus driver was ready to return to the ship, Jerry discovered a passenger Mrs Potter was missing and he asked all the "cousins" to organise a search for her. Nell and Fergus stayed close together while they looked around the giant fern plants in the jungle.

Suddenly they heard a faint cry for help in the greenery. They found the elderly lady sitting down holding her leg. "Help me" she said weakly "I've sprained my ankle and can't walk."

While Fergus struggled back through the jungle to the coach, Nell cared for Mrs Potter and made her comfortable until Jerry and the men passengers came to carry her back to the bus which raced back to the ship before it left port.

The Ship's doctor thanked Nell and Fergus and complimented Nell on her First Aid help. The next day Mrs Potter sent a box of chocolates to her two rescuers.

For the next fortnight the great Liner sailed eastwards on and on in the burning tropical sun to South America and more adventures.

Many passengers cooled off in the ship's two swimming pools.

Fergus and Nell chatted at the poolside with Mrs Potter who was resting her sprained ankle. A lady clambered out of the pool and sat down next to them.

Suddenly the lady gasped "Someone has stolen my bracelet. I left it here. Now it's gone."

She looked at the two children talking with Mrs Potter.

"You, girl" she pointed at Nell. "Have you got my bracelet?"

Nell was startled and confused. "No! I haven't" she protested.

The angry lady then wagged a finger at Fergus. "You, boy. Have you taken my bracelet?" Fergus looked dumbfounded and shook his head vigorously.

Mrs Potter was annoyed. "How dare you accuse my young friends. They've been with me. How dare you accuse them!"

While the two women argued, Fergus was so upset that he walked away to the pool to get away from the dispute.

Nell joined him in the pool and they swam around until suddenly Fergus disappeared by diving to the pool bottom. Then with a great splash he suddenly shot up to the surface holding a bright object.

"I've got it" he spluttered. "It was on the bottom of the pool."

He and Nell hurried out of the pool and rushed up to the angry lady who was still arguing with Mrs Potter.

"Here it is – here's your bracelet" Fergus panted breathlessly.

"Yes" gasped Nell "Fergus found it."

"Well done, Fergus" Mrs Potter smiled and congratulated him.

The angry lady stopped arguing. She looked embarrassed and speechless. Then she mumbled "Oh my, oh my. I must have lost it while swimming." She looked downcast "I don't know what to say."

Mrs Potter interrupted "You can apologise to them, apologise right now."

"I'm sorry children. I apologise."

"That's better" said Mrs Potter "Now you can take my young friends to the Ice-cream Parlour and buy them Sundaes."

"I will, I will" said the regretful lady who then took them for a treat.

Eventually the Liner reached the Panama Canal which crosses from the Pacific Ocean to the Caribbean Sea and the great ship squeezed through the narrow channel.

All the passengers lined the decks, marvelling as the ship eased slowly along the 50 miles long waterway without scraping its white painted hull.

After leaving the Canal the Liner picked up speed and surged through the Caribbean past shoals of flying fish to the next island stop of Aruba.

CHAPTER EIGHT

Under the Sea -Swimming with the Fish -Aruba

Aruba is at the top of the South American continent and it was once a Dutch colony. It still has a Dutch windmill and Dutch style colonial houses.

After exploring the capital town of Oranjestad "The Islanders" took an excursion to a tropical butterfly farm for breeding huge, dazzlingly colourful butterflies the size of birds.

Grandma, Mr Mac and Mother then took a once-in-a-lifetime voyage on the island's semi submarine, "The Seaworld Explorer", an underwater observatory with large port windows to study the amazing coral fields and shoals of tropical fish while sitting in the dry comfort below the sea.

Father took Nell and Fergus on a catamaran for snorkelling to explore the silent world of marine life in the warm crystal waters, to wonder at the treasures of the sea and marvel at the mysterious corals and swim over an old sunken shipwreck. The crew helped the children to put on the snorkels, masks and life jackets.

The fields of sponges on the seabed were the playgrounds for schools of Angel fish, blue tengs, barracudas, yellow fish and two feet long trumpet fish. The turtles were the stars of the ocean.

Above the surface, pelicans and frigate birds were diving into the water to catch fish.

The boatman on the snorkellers' catamaran gave Nell and Fergus bread to feed the fish which came and nibbled the children's fingers and toes when the bread was eaten. Snorkelling with fish and turtles was more exciting and more fun than splashing about in the ship's swimming pool. They were both glad they had learned to swim while at school.

After snorkelling, back on the catamaran the boatman served fresh fruit juices, slices of mangoes, pineapples and nuts before returning to the beach.

Back on the Liner at dinner everyone talked about their extraordinary adventures on the extraordinary island.

Nell wanted to send Postcards back to

Grandpa Anderson in Scotland but Grandma insisted that Nell also continue to write it all in her log-book for Grandpa during the next few days as the ship voyaged on to the next Caribbean island of Barbados.

Reading Nell's log-book of the warm south seas and tropical islands said Grandma would make Grandpa feel warm on the cold Scottish winter nights when they returned home. "And don't forget to write about me" said Fergus.

CHAPTER NINE

Making a Splash - Barbados

Nell and Fergus went to the Ship's Library to read all about Barbados, its history, the raids by Pirate Blackbeard on the Spanish gold laden ships and where to explore.

When the Liner anchored in the clear blue waters, the passengers boarded the ship's tender boats to ferry them ashore to the sun drenched beaches to disembark to explore the old colonial houses and the modern hotels and tourist shops.

Nell and Fergus ran along the bleached beaches and watched chattering yellow-tipped tailed monkeys in the water fringed palm trees, chasing colourful birds and large yellow butterflies.

At a beach Fruit Stall they bought glasses of fruit punch and ate banana bread.

A friendly Barbados boy Benji, leading a sleepy donkey stopped to talk to them about the Liner in the bay and their world voyage. Nell gave the dozy donkey some banana bread and Benji boy asked Fergus if he would like a ride on his old donkey he called "Lazybones".

As Fergus sat on the animal, old Lazybones seemed to wake up and shook his shaggy mane and floppy ears.

"Hold tight, hang on" shouted Benji as Fergus grabbed hold on the donkey's neck.

Without any warning except a bellowing snort and a furious braying roar, Lazybones sprang to life like a Jack in the Box. He reared up on his hind legs, kicking up a cloud of dusty sand and bolted off along the shore like a wild beast. Fergus' new straw hat was knocked off into the sea water.

Benji kept shouting to Fergus to "Hold tight, hang on" but the more Fergus clasped Lazybones' neck to cling on, the more the angry animal bellowed, bucked and bolted into the water. Then with a final snort the beast suddenly halted and off flew Fergus into the sea.

"Poor Fergus" called Nell as she ran to comfort her friend who was sitting in the water looking dazed.

Fergus shook the water out of his hair. "But I didn't do anything."

"I know" said Nell "He should be called "Lightning" not "Lazybones."

Benji held on to his animal who was now gentle, still and calm like the real Lazybones. "I'm so sorry, really sorry. Maybe Lazybones thought you were taking him back to the ship", he said. "Don't you call him Lazybones" scowled Nell "He should be called Lightning."

"Or 'Rocket'" grumbled Fergus as he got out of the water.

Nell gave him his crumpled, soaking straw hat and they walked back to the Fruit Stall for a fresh fruit juice.

"I'm not giving that Rocket donkey any more banana bread" said Nell as Lazybones nudged her, and Benji sliced a special wedge of melon for Fergus while Nell kept a watchful, suspicious eye on the unruffled, calm donkey who now looked more like a sleepy Lazybones

rather than Lightning. The two boys became very friendly. Fergus promised to send Benji a Postcard from Scotland.

Back on the Liner, Grandma wanted to know why Fergus' new straw hat looked so battered and soggy and he looked so bedraggled.

"Never mind" said Grandma adjusting her spectacles. "It's an interesting adventure for you to tell Grandpa in your log-book and put in Postcards to your Australian friends."

CHAPTER TEN

The Storm at Sea

After the ship cruised away into the night sky away from the warm Caribbean seas, the Captain set his course north on the long, last leg of the voyage to Southampton, the home port.

During the voyage the passengers amused themselves with entertainments.

Grandma earned applause by singing a Scottish song at a Karaoke and Mr Mac won a prize for guessing the number of miles the ship had sailed from Australia.

As the Liner steamed further into the colder Atlantic towards the Azores, these mid ocean Portuguese islands, the weather became wintry, the winds stronger and the tempestuous Atlantic waves thundered and crashed in foaming white breakers around the ship.

The Captain and his Officers on the Bridge peered through the foaming waves and sea spray trying to navigate a steady course.

The passengers abandoned the ship's dining rooms, the restaurants, games rooms, library and observation decks to retreat to the safety and comfort of their warm cabins.

Many passengers and crew became sea-sick as the ship pitched forwards, up and down and rolled sideways in the heavy swell and stormy seas under the blackening skies.

Mother, who had been a nurse, and Father comforted some of the passengers who had never experienced sea-sickness. They looked as ill as they felt as they clutched their sea sickness bags.

Granfer and Fergus returned to their cabin to ensure all their belongings were secured in place and were not being tossed about.

Grandma and Nell did the same to tidy up their books, souvenirs and clothes. They tried to write their Postcards and log-book but the ship was too unsteady for writing or reading, so they lay down on their bunks and chatted about the places they had visited, the people they had met, the odd collection of hundreds of passengers of various nationalities and backgrounds.

Nell to the Rescue

Darkness now fell much earlier as the ship steered northwards and the night sky became much darker north of the Equator.

"Time to sleep" said Grandma and she removed her spectacles and put on her nightgown.

"Lights out – God bless – Sleep well" added Grandma.

"Goodnight Grandma – sleep well."

Outside the snug cabin, the walls of sea water as high as a two storey house or a double decker bus crashed against the ship's hull as the Liner ploughed through the waves.

In the cabin bunk beneath her, Nell could hear her Grandma saying her prayers and reciting Psalm 107 "Some went down to the sea in ships, doing business on the great waters…"

The rest of Grandma's words were drowned out by a terrible, roaring growl, as a soaring wall of foaming sea crashed broadside against the hull of the ship that shuddered like a wounded whale.

Grandma quickly switched on the cabin light and called out "Are you alright, Nell? Never mind, we'll be alright."

Nell sat up and looked about the cabin which seemed in order. For a moment…until the next crash and smash by a monstrous wave that shuddered the ship and shattered the cabin window. The deafening noise, the sound of bursting glass and the gush of swirling water was made even more terrifying by the blackout of the electric light.

"Nell, Nell" Grandma shrieked "I can't see – I'm trapped."

When Nell swung herself out of the bunk she found she was standing in water up to her knees and walking on broken glass. She tried to make her way to open the cabin door but her way was blocked by heavy upturned furniture.

So she fumbled her way in the darkness to Grandma.

"Stay still, Grandma. I'll help you."

"Hurry, Nell, the water is still coming in – we'll drown soon. We must get out."

Nell could feel the heavy luggage case had fallen over Grandma's legs, trapping the old lady in her bunk as the water level was rising.

"We don't want to drown, Nell" she cried.

Nell forgot she was shivering, standing in very icy water with fingers so cold they were stiff like icicles.

"Never mind, Grandma. I'll get you out" and with one great heave, push and tug Nell pushed the luggage case off the tethered old lady. "Where are my glasses? I can't see."

"It's alright, Grandma – come and help me push this heavy chair away from the door."

Together they pushed and pulled at the weighty seat until there was enough space for Nell to climb over it and open the locked cabin door.

Outside she could hear people shouting and banging in the dark corridor.

"Help! Help! We're trapped" she shouted as she unlocked the door. A man's voice shouted "We're coming. We're coming" and slowly the door was pushed in to reveal a Ship's Steward with Father and Granfer all pushing the door inwards. The Steward shone his torch at Nell

and Grandma standing in the water in a cabin in chaos and water pouring in through the broken window.

Quickly the three men hauled Nell and Grandma from the flooded cabin, then closed the water-tight door and carried the two rescued survivors along the unlit dark corridor to an illuminated Rescue Room.

The officers quickly wrapped warm blankets around Grandma, who told them "Never mind me! You look after Nell. She saved my life. Nell saved me."

Everyone looked at Nell, who shyly pulled a blanket around herself until Mother May, Father, Grandfer MacSporran and Fergus all gathered around her as Grandma cried "Bless You, Nell."

The Rescue and Recovery Operation by the crew went as smoothly as the Lifeboat Practice Drills which had prepared the 2000 passengers and crew during the voyage.

And soon Grandma and Nell were given another cabin and moved in with all their salvaged possessions and souvenirs.

"I'm glad they found my glasses" said Grandma "I want to see where the ship is going!"

CHAPTER TWELVE

Safe on Dry Land

When the Liner docked at Southampton, a huge crowd of relatives, sightseers, radio and television crews were waiting and waving "Welcome Home" banners.

Father, Mother, Mr Mac and Fergus searched for Grandpa Anderson in the throng while Grandma and Nell were bombarded with questions by the radio, TV and Press reporters.

Grandma explained what happened in the storm and how Nell rescued her. Nell just smiled and said "I had to help Grandma" and she added "Please find Grandpa for me."

Soon Grandpa was found in the crowd and the next day the newspapers published photographs of Nell with the Andersons, MacSporrans and headlines "Nell, Ship's heroine rescues Grandma".

On the 'plane to Scotland "The Islanders" and Grandpa all agreed they were glad to be going home – even if it was a long journey to Scotland and their Island.

"Never mind" said Grandma "We'll soon be able to sleep in our own house and not worry about storms."

When they arrived back on their Island it was dark so Fergus and Mr Mac could see little of their new home until the morning and the Island of Surprises waiting for them.

The Islanders' Return

Nell's Scottish island could not be more different from Fergus' Australian home.

Nothing Fergus had heard about Nell's Western Isles had prepared him for the island's natural beauty and varied wildlife.

On the foreshore outside the Anderson's old stone house, Fergus marvelled at the untamed rocky landscape and the icy blue coastal waters unlike Australia's sunny golden sands and warm emerald ocean. The incoming tide tumbled waves of white rollers over the craggy rocks only a stone's throw from Nell's Atlantic House at the bay of Ellenabeich, the Island of Birches.

An otter scurried over the stony foreshore past the watchful eye of a grey heron while overhead a black cormorant flapped his wings then plunged underwater among the seaweed for fish.

An offshore seal raised his shiny black head with large wide eyes to watch Fergus in the morning haze.

Small boats across the bay were leaving the island, surging against the flood tide for the deeper ocean fishing grounds, to catch the fishermen's "Jewels of the Sea" and to drop the lobster creels.

Fergus breathed in deeply the fresh breeze with its tang of the seaweed and tasted the crisp saltiness of the sea foam on his lips.

Above the old house on the mist clad headland, sheep and deer grazed on the heather hillside while skywards seagulls noisily welcomed the sunrise and buzzards hunted rabbits.

Inland the farm folk were busy feeding chickens or calling their cattle or shepherding their flocks on the moors.

Looking about him, the island seemed to Fergus like a grey slate gemstone in the setting of crystal icy sea.

Fergus now understood why Nell and the Anderson family loved their island as they loved life. For him it was like the dawn, the start of a new life. He had found a new family in a new home in the old land of his forefathers.

Behind him, his Grandfather MacSporran and Nell walked across the beach to him. Granfer Mac put his hand on the lad's shoulder and said "Well laddie, what do you think of the auld country?"

Fergus smiled "It's great, it's great Granfer."

Nell giggled "I thought you would say dinkum."

As the old man and the two young friends walked homewards, Nell said "I told you Fergus. Dreams can come true."

At the house Fergus stopped at the door with its carved three linked L letters. "What's that?"

he asked. Nell explained it was her family's old talisman meaning "Life, Love and Laughter".

After breakfast, Fergus took a white stone from his pocket and put it on the fireplace mantel beside the Anderson family photographs. "I've brought this back from Professor Anderson's monument fountain in Sydney as a keepsake," he said.

Grandma clapped her hands with delight. "What a thoughtful lad you are."

Nell also had a present for Grandpa. "Here's my Voyage log-book for you Grandpa." Old Skipper Anderson clasped the diary saying

"I'll really enjoy reading of all your adventures."

Then Grandma explained it was time for the two MacSporrans to go over to meet Cousin Kate MacSporran at her Croft along the shore. As the two Grandfathers walked along the rocky path, they talked about Cousin Kate whom Granfer had not seen for 50 years. Fergus had never seen Granfer's cousin, Miss Kate.

Nell and Fergus followed. "What's Miss Kate like?" Fergus asked Nell. "Is she old and grumpy like Granfer?"

"No, no" protested Nell, "Aunt Kate is fun. She's like a real aunt. She lives in her old cosy Croft with her two cats. She's a painter with an artist's studio full of pots of paint and brushes and boxes of pencils and painters' things. It's a real artist's jumble but Grandma says painters are like that." Nell babbled on "And Aunt Kate enjoys exploring our islands in her boat. She's not like your Granfer. She's not so old and she's good fun."

Fergus was puzzled "Are they really cousins then?"

"Oh yes" said Nell "But they are as different as chalk and cheese, as different as Scotland and Australia."

Fergus had always envied Nell for having a Mother and Grandma. Now he has his own Great Aunt Kate who is fun, who likes exploring and has her own boat! Even before he met her Fergus felt he would like Aunt Kate. But would she like him?

So, as they arrived at the Croft, Fergus pulled up his socks, smoothed his hair and tried to look smart.

Aunt Kate greeted them in Gaelic saying "Ceud mile failte" – A hundred thousand welcomes! She was cheery with a big smile and laughing eyes. She hugged Fergus saying "So you are Fergus. You're a bonnie lad. It will be nice to have a young man staying here." She hugged him again and smelled of lavender as she showed Fergus and Granfer to their cosy rooms. Father said he would bring over their luggage later.

"I think the MacSporrans will all get along well together," Grandpa told Nell as they left the MacSporrans at the Croft and walked home.

"I hope Granfer doesn't upset Aunt Kate" said Nell. "Or the cats" said Grandpa.

Chapter Fourteen

Life on the Island

As the days got colder, Fergus was glad that Aunt Kate lit the log fire and knitted him a woolly scarf and gloves – especially on the morning he woke up to a white world of snow! Snow! Like small white leaves, like fluffy blossoms from the sky – like nothing he had ever seen in Australia.

He quickly dressed and ran outside to catch the snowflakes. Aunt Kate came out and laughed as she threw snowballs at him which he caught and rolled in his hands until his fingers felt too cold. So he ran back into the warm kitchen to warm his frozen fingers around a bowl of hot porridge.

Nell arrived at the Croft to help him make a snowman. Then she told him that next week they would have to go to the village school. Nell was smiling but Fergus just frowned – icy, frozen fingers, school – he wasn't sure which was worse.

The Headteacher, Miss Murray was more like Aunt Kate than Grandma. She smiled a lot and spoke Gaelic. Everyone happily welcomed Nell back but were more curious about Fergus, his accent and his Australia. Even worse were history and music lessons. He liked geography and arithmetic but there was no cricket. He longed for weekends.

Grandpa and Granfer took Nell and Fergus on Grandpa's fishing boat 'Iolaire' – Eagle – on trips to the islands of the Hebrides, to Mull, Scarba or Jura catching "Jewels of the Sea" to sell at Oban's fish market.

The old wooden boat was like old Skipper Grandpa – and weather-beaten by the blustery gales and stormy seas. 'Iolaire' was more like an old crow than an eagle. Nell explained 'Iolaire' is pronounced Yoolir in English.

As Grandpa and Granfer steered 'Iolaire' across the seas the two old seamen puffed on their pipes and told Nell and Fergus yarns of their boyhood on old sailing boats which they called "Maidens of the Wind".

While they were fishing off Mull, the ocean breezes dispersed the white clouds across the darkening skies. Fergus said "It looks like a storm coming." Grandpa nodded "Aye Shipmate, we'll batten down the hatches." Nell went into the cabin to get the oilskins.

When the rainstorm struck 'Iolaire' in the open seas the mountainous waves swept over the struggling craft which shuddered like a wounded animal.

The engine spluttered and coughed a cloud of smoke – then was lifelessly silent.

Skipper Grandpa ordered Nell into the wheelhouse while Granfer and Fergus tried to start the engine.

The boat drifted helplessly towards the rocks. Grandpa calmly tried to steer 'Iolaire' against the strong tide that would drag them to the dreaded

whirlpool of Corryvrecken, the graveyard of ships.

Overhead the seagulls' mournful wails reminded Fergus that Granfer Mac once told him that seagulls carried the souls of dead mariners. He had heard seamen say that Fair Winds are heaven-sent but storms are hell-sent.

Granfer dropped the anchor hoping to ride out the storm while Skipper Grandpa radioed May Day, May Day for assistance. A passing trawler quickly came to their rescue and towed the crippled 'Iolaire' like a lame duck instead of an eagle back to Ellenabeich.

Aunt Kate and Grandma welcomed them home with bowls of Scotch broth and mugs of cocoa.

Father Jack said it was time to get a new engine if Eagle wasn't to be a lame duck. But Grandpa said he couldn't afford it. So the menfolk spent the next few days trying to repair the engine while Nell and Fergus helped Grandma and mother to paint the old woodwork and tidy the cabin.

At home Grandma knitted woollen socks and gloves and Aunt Kate painted pictures to sell at the village shop to earn money for a new engine. Mother May worked as a District Nurse and Father Jack worked as a trawlerman.

Aunt Kate's Croft

Snow!

School

The lame duck!

51

A Picnic Misadventure

The Spring showers were like clouds crying tears in the skies and Nell and Fergus remembered the hot dry Australian days of sunbathing and shivered in their Scottish cloudbathing. As they trudged to school in their Wellington boots through the puddles, Fergus marvelled at the fields of bluebells, daffodils and primroses. "I've never seen such rain or colours" he said. Nell laughed. "We need the showers to give us the flowers" she replied.

When the warm summer weekends replaced the spring rains, Nell and Fergus collected foreshore driftwood for the wintertime fires and mussels for supper. Nell also liked to visit the old Croft and sitting on the old sofa in Aunt Kate's artist's studio watching paintings of the Islands come to life on the canvas.

Fergus couldn't even draw an apple so he kept away from the Studio and preferred helping Granfer to paint Aunt Kate's own boat the 'Dobhran' – the Gaelic for Otter and pronounced Dorran.

Fergus noticed a carved wooden plaque in the cabin in Gaelic saying "Nach uramach an Cuan" which Nell explained means "Whoever honours the Sea will be honoured".

At the weekend, Aunt Kate announced she needed fish, lobsters and to collect mussels to feed the menfolk. She and Grandma made up a picnic basket of fresh homemade scones, oatcakes, Scotch pies and bottles of homemade lemonade which they loaded onto 'Otter' with the lobster creels and fishing rods. The wind was set fair to sail them to Gull Island and Seal Rock and down the Sound of Shuna to the village of Toberonochy.

Kate quickly trimmed the sail and cast off the mooring while Grandma helmed the tiller and steered 'Dobhran' out into the open waters.

Fergus whispered to Nell "You never told me that Aunt and Grandma were sailors."

"I told you it's an Island of Surprises" said Nell. Kate's long white hair was streaming out like a pennant in the breeze – "Hoist the yards. Heave away my Jollies," she commanded in her

Skipper's voice to Fergus and Nell to hoist up the Mainsail. "Heave Ho my hearties" she ordered, as the wind filled the sail and 'Otter' sliced through the waves. These Islanders are also full of surprises thought Fergus.

"I hope we don't get dragged into the Corryvrecken whirlpool" he said.

"Never mind" said Grandma as she helmed the boat on its steady course. "You will soon hear it but you won't see it," as she steered 'Otter' away from the rocks.

All hands on deck worked as a team furling the sails, dropping the lobster creels and baiting the fishing lines. Soon they were catching mackerel and hauling the fish aboard.

"Grilled fish for supper tonight" said Grandma who was busily cleaning the mackerel with a Fisherman's knife and storing them in a bucket of sea water.

After anchoring 'Otter' in Gull Island inlet, they all took the inflatable dinghy to the island to collect mussels. While the two ladies unpacked the picnic basket, Nell and Fergus scoured the rocks for shellfish.

Suddenly Grandma yelled that the dinghy was floating out to sea! Aunt Kate ran into the water to try to catch hold of the dinghy but it was beyond her reach. Fergus and Nell ran down to the beach to help but the dinghy kept drifting away seawards.

As Aunt Kate and Grandma and Nell watched helplessly, Fergus pulled off his shirt and shoes and plunged into the sea. He swam through the swell to grab the drifting dinghy.

Nell and the two ladies clapped and cheered with relief as Fergus rowed back to the beach.

"I'm proud of you" said Aunt Kate as she dried Fergus with her shawl. "I know Australians are great swimmers but you swim like a dolphin!" Grandma wrapped him in the picnic table cloth and hugged him. She smelled of mackerel.

Nell looked serious – "I think I'm to blame. I forgot to tie up the dinghy. That's why it drifted away."

Grandma and Aunt Kate shook their heads "It's good that Fergus saved us. We could have been stranded here without a dinghy" said Grandma.

On the way back home Nell was quiet and still pondering about her mistake until Fergus said "Nell would have done the same as me – she is also a good swimmer."

That night at the Croft Aunt Kate and Grandma made a feast of grilled mackerel and boiled mussels and the Andersons and MacSporrans sang Gaelic songs while the two cats watched wide eyed until Grandma told everyone it was time for bed after such an adventurous day.

Grandpa put his hand on Fergus' shoulder saying "Thank you laddie for saving the ladies today." The old Scots Islander who was proud of his grandson added "Tapadh leat" – that means "Thank you" explained Grandpa.

Nell waved at Fergus and said "Mar sin leat" – "Bye." Then Nell added "Don't forget we'll have our school next term."

Fergus frowned "Ugh, don't talk about school" he muttered "I'd rather swim in the cold sea."

Nell laughed and said "Or we could go up to the mountains. To our Scottish Ben Nevis, our highest mountain!"

Fergus looked excited and happily agreed "Yes, yes. And we'll call our adventures "Nell of the Mountains."

Nell's Journey to Scotland...

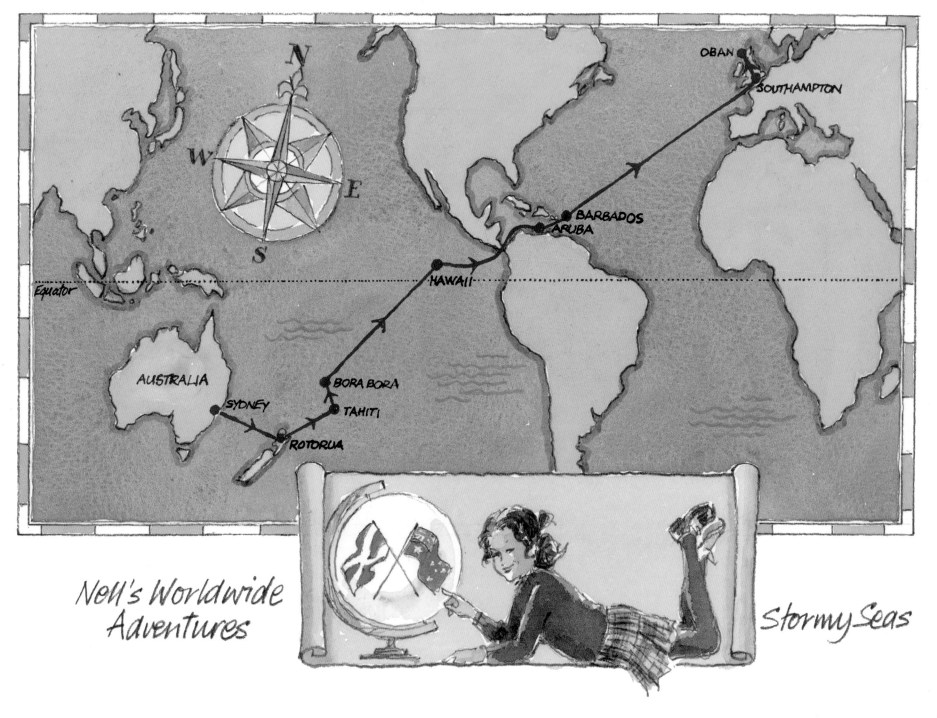

OBAN

SOUTHAMPTON

BARBADOS
ARUBA

HAWAII

Equator

AUSTRALIA

SYDNEY

BORA BORA

TAHITI

ROTORUA

Nell's Worldwide Adventures

Stormy Seas